INJURIES OF THE MIND

Injuries of the Mind

Forgiveness is possible

Pusonnam Yiri

AFRICA CHRISTIAN TEXTBOOKS

2017

Injuries of the Mind

© 2017 by Pusonnam Yiri

Africa Christian Textbooks (ACTS)

ACTS Bookshop, International HQ, TCNN,
PMB 2020, Bukuru, Plateau State, 930008, Nigeria
GSM: +234 (0) 803-589-5328; E-mail: info@acts-ng.com
Website: http://www.acts-ng.com

ISBN: 978-978-905-308-7 Print
ISBN: 978-978-905-309-4 ePub
ISBN: 978-978-905-310-0 Mobi

For further information, contact: 08105397509. Email: pusonnamyiri@gmail.com

DEDICATION

To the ministry of reconciliation to God.

CONTENTS

ACKNOWLEDGEMENTS

First, I am grateful to God for the grace to write. I appreciate my wife and children for their support.

I thank Dr. Nicholas Pwedon (late), who was one of the editors of the early version of the story of Twalbani years back. I am grateful to Rev. Jerry Faruk, Mrs. Janet Dann and Dr. William Paul Todd for excellent editorial input.

Further appreciation to all my partners and supporters in ministry.

INTRODUCTION

We are living in a world where there are different offences. You will one day be offended or maltreated no matter how careful you are. Handling such a situation can either help you grow effectively or harm you. When you choose to forgive, you will realize that indeed *there is someone's growth in forgiveness.* Both the giver and the receiver will experience relief that could enhance them in achieving the purpose of life.

I developed the seed idea of the story of Twalbani in 1995. I wrote a film script and a film titled *Good for Evil* was produced (Twalbani was named Jackson in the film). Subsequently, the script was converted into a novel manuscript. In the *Reconciliation Series,* it became necessary for me to combine the stories of Lisami and Twalbani into one for a reader to have a broad understanding of the subject matter. A few aspects of the early version of Twalbani's story were modified in this book.

You can overcome an offence by the grace of God.

CHAPTER 1

"They will kill me! Please, somebody help me!" Lisami, a girl of thirteen years old, slim, and dark in complexion cried, tears pouring down her face as she ran around the parlour looking desperately for a way out. Ntulo and Yansurili wanted to make sure she had received twenty strokes of the cane because she did not wash their children's clothes properly. Lisami had earlier received ten, but could not endure to the end, because this was the fourth time this week she was being whipped. The first time was two days ago, when they complained she did not sweep the parlour well. She was beaten by Yansurili with a stick. Some parts of her body were swollen and she sustained bruises on her back. The second time was some hours ago. Her offence was that she woke up late in the morning. Even though the beatings were not like the previous ones, the accumulation of pain was unbearable to Lisami. The third one was by Ntulo. He gave Lisami a hard beating because she did not clean his shoes properly.

Lisami used to be pampered by her parents in the village before they died. Her only aunt, Kunpira, who was supposed to help her, was not willing to shoulder the additional responsibility of paying school fees. She also had seven children to care for. Her husband, Chambasom, was not living up to his responsibilities. Lisami had to drop out of school, though the fee was not expensive. That was why, when Ntulo and Yansurili came to their village and her aunt informed her of their need for a house girl, she quickly accepted the offer and went to the city with them. Her hope was set on using the opportunity to go to school and eventually become a teacher. She was passionate about helping other children like her to have a sound education.

After listening to her dream, Ntulo and Yansurili promised her aunt their commitment in ensuring she obtained proper education. However, many things had changed since she came to the city. Ntulo and Yansurili broke their promise and turned her into a slave. Lisami worked night and day despite the fact that Ntulo and Yansurili's four children were old enough to do most of the work. Gandiban, the youngest among them was seventeen. Since her arrival, he often sneaked into her room at night and forced her to sleep with him. Lisami could not inform Ntulo or Yansurili for two reasons: Gandiban threatened to hurt her if she let the secret out; and she was not sure if Ntulo and Yansurili would believe her story.

In the past, she had never tried to run away from punishment, but the reverse was the case now because of the accumulated pain. Her shouting raised the neighbours' concern. Some of them had considered meeting Ntulo and Yansurili to talk to them. Only one had the courage to meet them. He was asked to leave the compound. They did not give him a listening ear.

Lisami was determined this time to be free from her misery. She ran out of the house towards the gate. Opening the gate was a big struggle, but she succeeded. She ran out of the compound, which was beside a main road. A motor cyclist almost hit her, but the rider was quick enough to avoid her. She did not bother about other possible risks of the road as she ran on and on, sobbing.

Nachau and his wife Akio were strolling in the direction of Ntulo's house. They were on their way to visit them. Nachau's house was within the area, about a kilometre away. They had known Ntulo and Yansurili for some years. They attended the same Church denomination and had been visiting Nachau for counselling.

It was a huge relief for Lisami when she saw Nachau and his wife. She also had known them in the Church. She grabbed Akio firmly and looked back, in case Ntulo and his wife were coming after her. Her body was shivering like a person struggling with fever. Her hair was like a mad woman's hair that has not been combed for a week. There were blood stains on her shirt, especially on her back.

"Please, help me," she pleaded. "They want to kill me!"

Akio held her tightly like a loving mother hen does to her chicks. She could feel Lisami's heart pounding as she cried and begged them to help her. "What is wrong with you?" Akio asked gently.

"Help me. I don't want to die!"

"You are safe now. I want you to tell me what is going on," Akio said. She squatted and looked at Lisami's face.

Nachau looked on with concern.

"Oga and Madam want to kill me," she stated.

"You mean Ntulo and Yansurili?" Akio inquired.

Lisami nodded.

"Why?"

Lisami continued to cry. She seemed unwilling to answer the question.

"We are on our way to visit Ntulo and Yansurili to discuss about you. We have heard of your situation. Let us go back to the house," Akio explained.

"I will not go back. They will kill me!" Lisami responded, struggling to free herself from Akio and run away.

"They will not kill you. We are sure by God's grace they will listen to us," Akio encouraged.

After prevailing on Lisami, she finally agreed to go to the house with them. When they reached the house, Lisami's fear returned. She started crying again. Akio continued to encourage her to be calm. When they opened the gate, fortunately, Ntulo and Yansurili were standing outside, discussing the situation.

"You are welcome," Yansurili said in pretence, looking at Lisami strangely. Nachau and Akio smiled. Lisami was hiding behind Akio.

"You are welcome to our house," Ntulo stated, forcing himself to smile.

"Thank you," Nachau responded on behalf of both of them.

"Please, let's go into the parlour," Ntulo said.

They all went into the parlour. Akio was holding one of the hands of Lisami. The others sat down, but Lisami remained standing.

"You can go to your room," Yansurili urged Lisami.

Lisami was reluctant to go.

"Go to your room!" Ntulo insisted harshly.

Lisami stared at Nachau and Akio, expecting them to speak.

"You can go," Akio said.

Quietly, Lisami walked to her room and shut the door. However, her ears were wide open to the conversation. Her room was close to the parlour.

"Where did you meet Lisami?" Yansurili asked.

"She ran into us on our way to your house," Nachau replied.

Ntulo looked on anxiously.

"What really happened? Why was she on the street crying?" Nachau inquired.

There was silence for a short time. Nachau and Akio waited patiently for Ntulo and Yansurili to speak.

"You are aware of how Lisami came to us," Yansurili said.

Nachau and Akio nodded.

"We tried to ensure Lisami is comfortable, but despite our efforts, she is not appreciative. She is lazy and grumbles anytime she is asked to work," Yansurili explained.

Lisami in her room was surprised at hearing what Yansurili said. It was as if she should rush out and call her a liar. She wondered why Yansurili would lie to protect her interest.

"We are fed up with her attitude and wish she had not even come to this house," Yansurili emphasized. "She has also developed the habit of stealing our money."

Lisami was confused in her room. She couldn't figure out the reason for their hatred of her.

"Concerning the stealing aspect, have you caught her red-handed?" Nachau asked.

There was silence again for a while. "We have not caught her, but we are sure our children would not steal from us," Yansurili answered.

"She is a little girl," Nachau remarked, even though he felt that Yansurili was not telling the truth. "Every young person is like a rising sun; you cannot know how bright it can turn out to be. God brought Lisami into this family for you people to support her."

Ntulo, Yansurili, and Akio listened.

"It is now that you have the chance to make a difference in her life," Nachau clarified.

"We thank you for the advice, but before she gets out of control, it is better we take her back to the village," Yansurili said.

"I don't think that is a good idea. Lisami needs you people to help her," Akio commented.

Nachau and Akio spent some minutes trying to convince Ntulo and Yansurili, but they refused to change their minds

"I would like to share a story if you will permit me. You can make your final decision after the story," Nachau suggested.

Ntulo and Yansurili looked at each other. "Okay," Ntulo reluctantly said.

"Thank you for the permission to share the story" Nachau stated.

CHAPTER 2

"This is a story of a boy called Twalbani. He was an only child to his parents. They showered love on him and wanted him to have a bright future," Nachau started the narration.

The parents loved each other dearly. In fact, they were role models to some couples in their community. Unfortunately, however, things became difficult after the death of his father.

Twalbani was ten years old when his father died. Two years later, his mother, Rikami, could not overcome depression as a result. In addition to the loss, some of her husband's relatives from the village came and took away most of her husband's possessions. They ignored her pleas for mercy and support. Rikami and Twalbani were sad over the actions of the relatives. Eventually, Rikami and her son suffered a lot. Paying the rent of the small apartment they were occupying also became difficult.

Rikami's blood pressure was often on the rise. Her doctor advised her severally against worrying, but she refused to be comforted.

One day, Rikami and Twalbani sat on a mat under tree and were eating food. Rikami was not looking well. Twalbani asked her about her health, but she was quiet. Suddenly, she slumped. Earlier, she had spent about an hour before dawn crying. Her burdens continued to weigh her down.

Twalbani, in tears, after giving her a helping hand, rushed to call Eram, a neighbour who had been helpful to them since the death of Twalbani's father. Eram and his wife attached much emphasis to showing kindness to anybody who needed it. The wife was not home when Twalbani arrived. She had gone to the market for her usual business of selling grain. Twalbani found Eram eating food. He quickly stopped eating and washed his hands as soon as he got the news. They rushed to Rikami anxiously.

"Mama Twalbani!" Eram called desperately immediately they came to her.

Rikami did not answer.

Eram called again, but she was still quiet.

"Twalbani," Eram called.

"Yes, sir," Twalbani answered in distress.

"Take care of your mother; let me go and get a taxi," Eram said, rushing out of the house.

Twalbani, while crying sat down on the mat and put his mother's head on his lap. "Please, Mummy, don't die. I love you!" he exclaimed, a flood of tears rolling down his cheeks.

Eram came back with a taxi after some minutes. He rushed to Rikami and lifted her into the car with support from Twalbani and the taxi driver.

When they reached the hospital, the doctors and nurses were efficient in giving her emergency treatment. After about two hours, she regained consciousness.

Many of her neighbours and friends visited her at the hospital. Gawi was also informed. She was Rikami's younger sister and married to a businessman named Puranza. They had three children.

Gawi and her husband came to the hospital and paid some money for Rikami's treatments. Gawi stayed in the hospital with Twalbani. He was asked to return home and live with Eram, but he refused. He insisted on staying close to his mother.

Rikami was taken to a general ward on admission after her condition had improved.

At night, Rikami asked Gawi to sit on a chair beside her bed while Twalbani sat on the bed also beside her.

"I am still not feeling well. Just in case I don't make it; I request that you take care of Twalbani. He should live with you. That is the only favour I ask of you," Rikami said faintly.

"Don't be negative. You will recover and be healthy again," Gawi encouraged.

Rikami nodded gently and closed her eyes.

Gawi sensed that her posture on the bed was abnormal. She touched her, but there was no positive response.

Twalbani was confused. He shook his mother, but she did not wake up.

Gawi ran and called one of the nurses and a doctor. They came and tried to revive her, but it was too late.

"We have lost her," the doctor told Gawi after confirmation.

Gawi started crying.

"Aunty, is she dead?" Twalbani asked anxiously.

Gawi nodded.

"No…!" Twalbani shouted, collapsing on his mother and wept bitterly.

Other patients and their relatives in the ward looked on in sympathy.

*

After the funeral, Twalbani lived shortly with one of his father's distant relatives in the city. Gawi then came and picked him. He thought deeply about the idea of staying with his aunt for the first time. He became confident that she would take good care of him considering how she had related earlier when she visited them. She used to buy him some candies and toys.

The drive to the house took them some minutes. When they arrived, the gateman opened the gate and welcomed them as Gawi drove into the compound. The children who were watching a film in the parlour heard the horn of the car and rushed out of the house to welcome them.

The compound was calm and peaceful. Birds were making sweet melodies.

The children ran and embraced their mother first before Twalbani, immediately they alighted. Puranza was not at home. He had travelled two days ago on business.

"You are welcome, Twalbani," Ndabo, the eldest and only male child in the family said. He was one year older than Twalbani. The two girls, Sunzuro and Omale also came and welcomed him.

Ndabo opened the boot and picked Twalbani's bag to his room and returned to meet the rest in the parlour. "Mummy, Twalbani's room is dirty," Ndabo said.

"We will take care of it later," Gawi replied.

After some minutes of discussion, Gawi stood up to lead Twalbani to his room. Based on the way he was welcomed, he was happy that his stay would be wonderful.

Gawi opened the door as soon as they reached the room. The mattress on the bed was small and old. The bed sheet on it was also not too clean. "This is your room."

"Thank you. I am very grateful."

"You are welcome. Lunch will be ready soon," Gawi stated and walked away.

Twalbani found a place to keep his bag and shoes. Quickly, the condition of the room sent a negative signal to him. "Was she not expecting me?" he thought aloud.

Later, Gawi sent for him. He went to the dining room and ate his food. It was delicious. He thanked his aunt and commended her cooking. Gawi smiled in response.

Throughout the night, sleep was difficult for Twalbani. He battled with mosquitoes. Early in the morning, at 6am, Gawi walked into his room and stood beside him. She had tied a wrapper around her chest on top of her nightgown. She looked at him strangely, while he turned from side to side for comfort.

"Wake up!" she shouted.

Twalbani reluctantly woke up. "Good morning," he greeted her, rubbing his eyes with his hands.

"It is time for you to wake up and help me in the house with some work! As from today, you should make sure you always wake up before 6am!"

"Please, let me rest for some minutes. I couldn't sleep well because of mosquitoes."

"Rest?" Gawi reacted. "Let's go outside so that you can wash my children's clothes." She forcefully dragged him out of bed.

The weather was cold. It was the first time that Twalbani had washed so many clothes. His mother only let him wash some of his own clothes on a few occasions.

Gawi came out holding more clothes. When she reached him, she dropped the clothes on him. "Make sure you finish washing these clothes before ten o'clock. I only want hardworking people around here."

Twalbani removed the clothes she dropped on him. He raised his head and looked at her. "Please, let me eat first. I am hungry."

"Did I hear you say you are hungry?" she reacted angrily, holding one of his ears.

"That hurts!" he shouted.

"In my house, you must work before you eat. Before I come out again, I want to see you washing." She let go his ear and walked away.

Twalbani stood helplessly, watching her going. He wondered why her change of attitude towards him. He reluctantly continued washing the clothes. The washing took him about three hours. Gawi had forced him to repeat some clothes she felt were not properly washed.

Twalbani felt weak after the washing. He went to his room to rest as he contemplated the experience. Suddenly, he heard a call. He stood up and rushed out of the room.

"Twalbani!" Gawi called again.

"Yes."

"Come and take your food."

"Okay," he went and picked his food.

Gawi's children were sitting at the dining table eating rice and chicken. The youngest daughter, Omale, shared her meat with her dolly in a playful manner.

Gawi walked out of the kitchen to the dining room to fill some empty bottles with water from the filter close to the table.

Twalbani held his food in a plate. It was different from Gawi's children's food. His own was of low quality. Gawi claimed to love her children so much. Four years after her wedding, she was childless until the fifth year. Those years of childlessness were terrible experiences Gawi would never forget.

Twalbani focused on his own food, as he walked to the table. Gawi's children turned and looked at him. Immediately he reached the table, he drew out one of the chairs and sat down.

"Mummy, why is Twalbani's food different from ours?" Ndabo asked curiously.

"Shut up! Do you think you love him more than I do?" Gawi shouted at her son.

Ndabo kept quiet.

"Twalbani, go to your room and eat!" Gawi said aggressively.

Twalbani fearfully took his plate of food and rushed to his room. Immediately he entered, he put the plate of food on the mat and sat down to eat. He was crying as he ate. He wondered why his aunt stopped him from using the table. "Why then did she earlier allow me to use it?" he asked himself.

Gawi later invited her children to her room and warned them against showing kindness to Twalbani. "His mother did not love me. She was often against me. She even advised me against marrying your father when he came to me for marriage" Gawi stated.

The children listened.

"Twalbani is only here because I could not reject his mother's last wish," Gawi emphasized.

"Mummy, it is not proper for us to treat him badly," Omale said.

"I agree with Omale," Ndabo commented.

"Then you have to choose between him and me. I will not take it lightly with any of you if you don't obey me. He is not to be treated as a member of this family!" Gawi remarked angrily.

The children kept quiet and thoughtful.

*

In the morning, the day after, Gawi came out and sat down in the parlour, and put the money she was holding on the table in front of her. The house was quiet. Her children had gone to school. "Twalbani!" she called, making some arrangements on the settee.

"Yes!" Twalbani answered, walking into the parlour to meet her.

"Come here quickly and let me send you to the market."

"Here I am," Twalbani fearfully said, while squatting before her.

"Do you know where the main market is?"

"I was there five times with my mother."

"Okay, take this money and buy some soup ingredients for me. Take good care of the money," Gawi stressed, while handing the money and the list of items on a piece of paper to him.

"I will." Twalbani stood up and walked quickly to the door.

"Where are you going to put the ingredients? On your head, or in your mouth? You are going without carrying a bag!"

"I forgot," Twalbani remarked, holding his head.

"Useless boy, you can't even think for yourself! Go into the kitchen and pick a bag in the cupboard."

"Okay."

Twalbani went and picked the bag. On his way to the market, he felt calmness outside Gawi's house. When he was about to enter the market, he met with a group of garage boys. They specialized in stealing from people at the market, especially those passing through the main gate.

They attacked Twalbani, beat him up and stole all the money he had with him. People stared at the scene without making any effort to help him.

Many people were afraid of the boys. They attacked anyone who tried to help even more than their first victim. The State Government had tried to arrest all of them, but had not succeeded. Most of the boys were school drop-outs. They called themselves "Kururu boys."

After robbing Twalbani, they left him lying helpless on the ground. He sustained an injury on his forehead. Blood gushed onto his face and chest, staining part of his shirt, which was torn into rags.

"Please, sir, help me! They have stolen my money. If I don't take home what my Aunty asked me to buy, she will beat me! Help me!" Twalbani begged, holding the leg of a passer-by.

"Leave me alone!" the passer-by shouted impatiently.

Despite a lot of efforts to get help from people, Twalbani was unsuccessful. He stood up in distress, wondering what to do next. What am I going to tell Aunty? Will she believe my story?" he pondered. "Oh God, help me!" Twalbani cried loudly, while picking his bag from the ground.

When he reached home, he found Gawi reading a novel in the parlour. She loved reading in her leisure time. He walked towards her holding an empty bag.

"What happened to you?" she asked curiously.

"Twalbani sobbed, squatting before her. "I could not get what you sent me to buy. As I was about to enter the market, a group of boys attacked me, and stole the money you sent me with. That was where I got this injury," he explained.

"Stole the money?" Gawi kept her novel beside her and stood up. "Does that mean you have given my money to those garage boys just like that?"

"Have mercy on me! I did not do it deliberately," Twalbani pleaded, crying loudly, with blood still gushing out from his forehead.

"You have gotten what you deserved. Come here!" Gawi ordered, holding him firmly.

"Forgive me!"

She held him with her left hand and beat him with the right hand. "Next time, you will be very careful when I send you to the market," she warned, abandoning him on the ground, crying from the pain of both injury and punishment.

After some minutes, Twalbani stood up and went out of the house to the nearest clinic and was treated. He felt dizzy after the treatment. He went to his room, thinking about his dead parents and crying. As he was about to lie down on the bed to rest, he heard a loud call from Gawi, who was still in the parlour. He quickly stood up, wiping his tears because of the fear that Gawi could beat him again if she saw him crying.

As soon as Gawi saw him, she noticed the plaster on his forehead. "Yee!" she shouted. "You are a thief!"

Twalbani moved backward in confusion.

"Who gave you the money for the treatment? I am sure you kept some part of my money for yourself."

"Someone gave me a gift of two thousand Naira after the funeral. I used three hundred Naira for the treatment."

"So, you have some money and you did not tell me? Go and bring the remaining amount?"

"Okay," Twalbani replied reluctantly.

"I will keep it for you. Anytime you need it you should ask me."

"Okay," Twalbani stood up and ran to his room to get the money. When he came out, he handed it to her.

"That's very good. You should go and wash the plates before you eat."

Twalbani walked away tiredly to the kitchen and after one hour he finished washing the plates before Gawi gave him his food.

CHAPTER 3

Gawi and the children sat in the parlour. She was watching a film while Omale and Sunzuro were playing a game. Ndabo was reading a book. Omale shouted excitedly after defeating Sunzuro in the game. Gawi told her to keep quiet and not to disturb her concentration on the film. Suddenly, the horn of a car was heard. Gawi turned to confirm through a window. "Your father is back!"

The children ran out to meet him. After welcoming him, Ndabo, carried his bag and followed the rest into the house. Puranza held Sunzuro and Omale to himself, on their way to sit in the parlour.

"Daddy, I hope you have not forgotten to buy my ball?" Ndabo asked, on his way with the bag to his father's room.

"I have not forgotten. It's in the bag," Puranza assured his son, as he turned to Gawi. "Dear, how are things in the house?"

"Everything is fine. How was your journey?" Gawi inquired while getting a bottle of water from the refrigerator.

"It was fine, except for the engine problem the car developed on the way."

"That is bad," she responded, as she took the water and a cup to him.

After drinking, there was a moment of silence. Puranza was playing with Omale.

Twalbani came out, still with the plaster on his forehead. "You are welcome, sir," he said, while squatting before him.

"Thank you. How are you doing?"

Twalbani was quiet. He focused on the horrible way Gawi was looking at him.

Puranza noticed the mood of Gawi. "What happened to your forehead?" he asked, stroking the place caringly with his right hand.

"I was injured by a group of boys at the main market when Aunty sent me to buy some things."

"You and who went to the market?" Puranza inquired curiously.

"Alone," Twalbani answered carefully.

"Dear, why did you send him alone to the market?" Puranza asked.

"I needed him to help!" Gawi reacted harshly.

"It is not right for him to go alone," Puranza said.

Gawi was silent.

"Do you go to school?" Puranza asked, ignoring the mood of Gawi.

"I withdrew after the death of my mother."

Puranza was quiet for a moment. "We will see what we can do about it. You can go to your room now."

"Thank you, sir," Twalbani stood up and hurried to his room.

"It was wrong for you to ask him the question about school. You should have asked me?"

Puranza listened.

"What do you intend doing about his school?"

"We need to send him to school soon."

"It will be a burden on us if we send him to school soon. Let him stay at home for some months!" Gawi responded aggressively.

"My dear, let us treat him properly."

"No! I don't think that is a good idea."

"Let's leave this matter for now. I am going out to see a friend. I promised to see him immediately I returned from the journey."

"That's better!"

Puranza stood up, went out to his car and drove away.

Two days later, he travelled again.

Gawi and the children were sitting in the parlour when they heard a knock on the door. When Gawi opened the door reluctantly, she saw a man with the gateman. The man was dark in complexion, wearing a suit and dark glasses.

"You are welcome," she stated.

"Thank you. Are you Mrs. Puranza?"

"Yes. Is there any problem?" Gawi demanded, drawing closer to him.

"Madam," he said, removing his identity card from the left pocket of his suit and showing it to her. "I am from the Police Station."

"What can I do for you?"

"I have been sent to inform you that your husband had an accident this afternoon."

"Accident!" Gawi exclaimed, looking very worried. She held the Policeman firmly. "What happened to him?" she inquired in anxiety.

"I'm afraid that he died as a result."

Gawi held her head with her hands, screaming, and fell on the ground rolling. Her children, who had overheard their discussion, also came out crying and holding their mother.

"Take it easy, Madam," the Policeman said.

Twalbani also overheard the discussion. He came out crying over the tragedy and thinking about how good Puranza would have been to him.

*

Twalbani was facing more serious challenges seven months after the death of Puranza. He had no new clothes to wear. His old clothes were torn and he was thin. He sat on a mat wearing a singlet. He turned, picked his bag, and removed his family's picture. It was the picture of himself with his parents when he was two years old.

Immediately he looked at the picture, he started shedding tears, holding firmly to it in love and loneliness. "Oh Mummy and Daddy, if only you were alive, I wouldn't have experienced this hardship!" he lamented, as he kissed the picture, his tears falling on it. "Mummy, how I wish you could see how I am suffering at the hands of the person you trusted. I really miss and love you, Mummy and Daddy," he stated. "Please, God, since I can't have my parents back, kindly give me a family that will love me," he prayed.

He hoped God would answer his prayer. He remembered his mother teaching him that it is important to pray to God in good or challenging times.

*

Twalbani had a headache. He was unable to do some of the work in the house as early as he was expected to. When he entered the parlour in the afternoon, Gawi, who was busy reading a story for her daughter, Omale, called him sharply.

"Yes," Twalbani answered, turning immediately in fear, because anytime she called him like that it meant trouble.

"Have you washed the plates?"

"That is what I am going to do now."

"You mean since the time we finished eating, those plates are still dirty?"

"I was tired and not feeling well, that's why I decided to rest for a while before I washed them."

"Come here!" she shouted angrily.

When he came closer to her, she held one of his ears and pulled it. "Next time, no matter what is wrong, you have to finish my work first before any excuse."

"Okay," he stated in pain.

"Make sure you wash them properly, not like yesterday," Gawi said, pushing him to the ground away from her.

He went into the kitchen looking sad. In the process of washing, one of the plates slipped from his hand and dropped on the floor. Knowing what would happen to him, he quickly started picking up the pieces with his hands.

The sound of the broken plate got the attention of Gawi. "Twalbani! What happened? Did I hear the sound of a broken plate?"

Twalbani couldn't answer. After a moment of silence and picking up the pieces of the broken plate, he came out of the kitchen in tears. One of his fingers was bleeding. He had injured himself in the process of picking the pieces of plate. He held in his hands some of the pieces as he approached Gawi.

"You idiot! You broke my plate because of your usual carelessness!"

"It was a mistake," he said, while moving backward from her.

"Come here!" she ordered, as she stood up and removed a radio cable. "Just wait till I catch you!"

Twalbani begged her repeatedly to have mercy on him.

Gawi held him tight, ignoring his pleas. She beat him with the cable furiously, until he almost lost consciousness. In tears and pain, he lay helpless on the floor.

"Next time, you will know how to take good care of my things. As a punishment, I am going to use your money with me to buy a new plate!"

*

The next morning, the weather was cold and Gawi's compound was quiet. Twalbani was on the bed crying and shivering. The bed sheet he covered himself with was torn and still old.

When Gawi came out of her room at 7am, she saw that Twalbani had not done his morning duties. She walked to his room, suspecting that he might still be sleeping. "You have to work first before you rest," she said, while shaking and lifting him up to stand on his feet.

Twalbani could not stand. He fell back painfully on the bed.

"Stand up, or must I use a cane on you?"

"Aunty. I am ill. Please, take me to the hospital!" he pleaded faintly.

"I cannot waste my money on you at the hospital."

"You should use the money I gave you."

"Have you forgotten the plate you broke yesterday? I will use the money to buy a plate."

"Help me, for God's sake!" he begged, crying bitterly and shivering.

Gawi kept quiet for a moment. She stood up and went out of the room. She brought some pain relieving tablets and gave them to him with a cup of water.

Twalbani sat up to take them. After he had swallowed the tablets, she snatched the cup forcefully just before he gave it back to her and walked out of the room.

*

After some hours, there were light rains. Twalbani was still lying on the bed. Gawi walked in and sat on the bed beside him. She stared at him in silence for a short time.

Her silence made him curious and more fearful.

"Twalbani."

"Yes, Aunty," he answered calmly.

"I cannot afford to continue keeping you here. I am tired of your problems. I want to focus on supporting my children without any distraction from you."

The announcement pierced deep into Twalbani's heart. He looked at his Aunty thoughtfully. Slowly, tears rolled down his cheeks, as he wondered why she hated him. "Be patient with me," he begged earnestly.

"I have done my best and I think my best is enough. You have to leave!" Gawi shouted angrily.

"I am ill. I can't walk well. Even if you will send me away, kindly allow me to recover first. I beg you in the name of God. Help me!"

"No!" she reacted, standing up. "Leave now or I force you out. I hate seeing you in this house. I hate you!"

"Aunty, please!" he pleaded continuously in tears.

Gawi refused to accept his pleas. She gave him a little amount of money for transportation and dragged him out with his bag into the rains.

"Don't come back to this house. Leave me and my family alone with our problems." She shut the door, leaving him outside on the ground still crying and begging her.

Within some minutes, he was wet. He could hardly stand up to pick his bag. When he finally stood up after a big struggle, he walked to the gate, falling and getting up. On reaching the gate, he turned and looked at the house, wondering where he could possibly go.

CHAPTER 4

As passers-by discussed day-to-day activities, Twalbani lay on a carton in front of a big house owned by one of the wealthy men in the State. He was still feeling terrible.

Crying and feeling weak, he slowly stood up to his feet. Despite looking all around him there was no one to help him. He tried to walk across to the other side of the road. Suddenly, a speeding car came and knocked him down. He fell bleeding from his face and sustained a fracture in his left leg.

Mwashat, the car's owner, opened the door and rushed out. Immediately he reached Twalbani, he bent down and examined him carefully. His face was sad, as he turned around to call his driver. The driver was quite upset by the incident. It was the first time he had ever knocked someone down.

"Come here quickly and let us take him to the hospital."

"Okay, sir," the driver replied, rushing to help.

Mwashat was a well-educated, wealthy man who loved the Lord. He was respected in his community because of his kindness, love, humility and concern for the needy.

At the hospital, Twalbani lay on the bed still unconscious. Doctors had already attended to his wounds. The senior doctor who owned the hospital came into Twalbani's room with Mwashat. He went to his file, picked it up and read it through to assess his condition. Mwashat looked disturbed. "Doctor, how is he? Will he be okay?"

"Yes, he will be okay by the grace of God."

"Do all you can to ensure he gets better. Don't worry about the bills, I will settle everything."

"Okay, sir," the doctor said and left the room.

Troubled over the condition of the poor boy, Mwashat moved closer to him when he noticed a sign of recovery.

"Where am I? What happened to me?"

Mwashat sat on a chair beside him and helped to calm him down. "You had an accident involving my car and I brought you to this hospital for treatment."

Twalbani cried out in pain. He looked at Mwashat and the room, which were strange to him.

"You should rest. My name is Mwashat."

Twalbani slept and woke up after an hour. Mwashat was still beside him.

"What happened? Why were you crossing the road like that?"

Touched by the question, Twalbani started crying. He narrated the story of his experiences with Gawi.

Mwashat felt sad over the story. He held one of the hands of Twalbani. "Don't worry. I will contact your aunt and talk to her."

"I doubt if she will listen to you."

"Give me her address."

Twalbani gave Mwashat the address.

"Have a good rest. I will go now and discuss with her."

"Okay, sir."

Mwashat went to Gawi's house. It was not too difficult to trace the house. She welcomed him happily, but her mood changed when he mentioned his reason for the visit and the condition of Twalbani. Gawi refused to change her mind about Twalbani despite pleas from Mwashat. She asked him to let Twalbani live with him when he is discharged from the hospital pending her final decision.

After further discussions, she agreed to go with him to the hospital to see Twalbani. Mwashat collected her phone number and together they went to the hospital. Her stay there was brief. She went back home contemplating her next move.

Mwashat bought some new clothes for Twalbani. After two weeks at the hospital, Twalbani was discharged. Gawi did not visit again. Mwashat paid the bills. He dialled Gawi's line twice, but there was no connection.

Mwashat went to her house before taking Twalbani out of the hospital, but did not meet her. He decided to take Twalbani to his house pending the final outcome of his meeting with her.

From the hospital, Mwashat took Twalbani in his expensive car. For Twalbani, it was like a dream, seeing himself in a car he had never thought of entering.

As they went into Mwashat's compound, Twalbani was excited by the beauty of the place. The rows of magnificent and well-arranged flowers and the compelling scenery got his attention. The compound was looking calm and peaceful, with birds singing in the trees.

When the driver had parked the car, Mwashat came out and opened the door for Twalbani and helped him out of the car. They assisted him to his room and laid him on the bed. It was the first time he had seen such a beautiful room.

"You should rest. We will talk later," Mwashat said.

"Okay, sir," Twalbani stated.

Mwashat smiled.

"Thank you," Twalbani said gratefully. "God will reward you for your kindness."

"Glory to God," Mwashat remarked, while leaving the room.

Mwashat's cook later brought a delicious meal to Twalbani. He ate with satisfaction.

After he had eaten, Mwashat walked into the room and sat on the bed beside him. "How are you feeling now?" he asked gently.

"I am getting better. Thank you for the food."

Mwashat smiled.

"Sir, where is your wife?"

"I am still single. One day, by the grace of God I hope to be married."

"Okay. I will pray that God will give you a wife who is as good as you."

"I am happy to hear that."

"I know it is not easy for you to assist me. You are a kind person and different from my aunt."

"I give God the glory. Whatsoever assistance I give to anybody, whether known to me or not, is like doing it to Jesus. Tell me of what you know about Jesus."

"Only a little. I know that Jesus loves me," Twalbani responded.

"It is because of love that He came and died for your sins and mine."

"What is sin?" Twalbani asked curiously, with a bit of confusion on his face.

"That's a good question. Sin means to miss the mark or to disobey God."

Twalbani looked more curious. Mwashat realized it.

"You and I in our words, thoughts and actions have wronged God. The only way to deliver us from the wages of sin was for Him to send His Son, Jesus, to pay the price we couldn't pay ourselves. He died in our place, and then rose from the dead. The most important thing is to first accept Jesus to be your Lord and Saviour putting all your trust in Him to help you."

Mwashat further explained the good news about Jesus to Twalbani. They held hands eventually and prayed. Twalbani accepted Jesus. He felt great peace and happiness in his heart.

Four days later, Mwashat finally met with Gawi. She insisted that Twalbani will not live with her again.

Mwashat told her of his intention for Twalbani to continue living with him. She quickly gave her approval, but advised him to also contact Twalbani's paternal relatives for their consent.

A day later, Gawi and Mwashat went to the village and discussed with Twalbani's paternal relatives. It was a difficult decision to make, but since they didn't want to be effectively responsible for Twalbani's upbringing, they finally gave their approval. Mwashat was glad with the decision. He didn't want to lose Twalbani.

Mwashat introduced Twalbani to some of his relatives. They accepted him into the family, but further encouraged Mwashat to marry.

CHAPTER 5

Gawi's children had gone to school. She loved coming back home from the office before them to prepare their meal. However, this time was different. Gawi sat on a chair in the parlour crying and looking distressed. "Oh my God!" she wept. "What have I done to deserve this?"

Suddenly, Usoko, her friend walked in and sat beside her. She held Gawi with her left hand for encouragement. Usoko had been a long-time friend to Gawi. She was good at encouraging her in times of need.

"Gawi," Usoko called twice, but no answer.

Gawi was still crying. She looked at Usoko in tears. Her eyes had swollen.

Usoko waited for her to speak.

"I am really in trouble!"

"What happened?" Usoko asked anxiously.

"An amount of money went missing in our office. Five of us working in the office have been dismissed," Gawi explained, shedding more tears. She lay on the shoulder of Usoko and held her firmly. "I am in trouble, Usoko. I am seriously in trouble."

"Stop crying and calm down. We will see what we can do about it."

Gawi could not be easily comforted. She wept loudly for about thirty minutes. Usoko almost lost patience, but was motivated by friendship. Eventually, she prevailed on her to be quiet.

*

Two years after her dismissal, Gawi and her children were in a terrible situation. Feeding the family had become a huge challenge. She sold most of their valuables cheap just to raise some money.

One afternoon, Gawi and her children were sitting in the parlour discussing what to do next. Her son, Ndabo, was busy cleaning his torn shoe and her two daughters were sitting close to her. Suddenly, they heard a bang on the door. They quickly turned in its direction, wondering what was wrong. As they stared, the door was forcefully opened. Two muscular young men in sunglasses walked in.

Gawi stood up, thinking they were armed robbers. "If they are armed robbers, what do they want from us?" she thought.

As she was thinking, she saw another man dressed in colourful native wear walking in towards them from behind the young men. After a careful look at his frowning face, she realized he was their landlord. Remembering the notices she had earlier received from him about the rent, she quickly felt that they were in trouble.

Gawi started shaking and walking towards the landlord, while her children held each other fearfully.

"Welcome, sir," she said.

"Thank you!" the landlord replied angrily. "You must leave my house today! I am tired of keeping you here with debts!"

"Please, sir," Gawi knelt down and held his legs. "Have mercy on us. Even food is difficult for us to afford. We have sold most of our valuables to survive, but still there is no effective solution to our problems. If you send us out of this house, we don't have any place to go!"

As Gawi was begging, Usoko walked in, surprised by what was happening.

"No matter what you do, you have to leave this house today." The landlord insisted, pushing Gawi away from him. "Remove their things!" he instructed the young men.

"Have mercy on us!" Gawi cried louder, while the young men removed their things.

"For God's sake, help us, sir!" Omale begged, holding her brother and sister together in tears.

"Please, Usoko, help us in begging the Landlord," Gawi turned to Usoko and requested desperately.

"Kindly give her time; she will settle with you later, I am very sure," Usoko quickly said "Consider her problems," she added.

The landlord refused to do as they had requested. His patience had been tried. He had allowed them to live in the house without paying rent for one year.

The parlour looked scattered. The two young men came back and dragged Gawi out, after taking her possessions out of the house. Gawi wept and begged repeatedly as they dragged her.

Gawi, her children and Usoko were all forcefully ejected. The landlord locked the door and walked away with the young men.

"We are finished!" Gawi lamented.

"Stop crying, Gawi," Usoko said, patting her on the shoulder. "Since the day you mentioned your rent problem, I have been thinking of talking to one of my friends. She has an empty room in one of her houses. I will convince her to let you occupy it. You can live there for a while," she explained.

"Help us, Usoko! I don't know what to do!" Gawi begged.

"No problem. I will talk to her," Usoko assured her. She stood up, and tidied most of the scattered items.

Gawi and the children continued to cry.

Suddenly, the weather changed. After a few minutes, it started to rain heavily. Gawi, her children, Usoko and most of their possessions were soaked. A flashback of what happened when she threw Twalbani out crossed her mind. She took a deep breath to calm herself.

*

Usoko's discussion with her friend was successful. The house was located in a remote area of the state, near a huge, stinking refuse container. Heaps of refuse were often there without being removed by the men of the environmental sanitation agency. Pigs and goats often visited the place in search of food.

Gawi and her children eventually relocated to the house. It seemed strange to them, but there was no other better alternative. It felt like a nightmare. They had never thought of living in such a place.

"Thank you very much, Usoko. If not for you, I wouldn't have known what to do," Gawi said sadly, while sitting on a bed with one of her daughters and Usoko. The other two children sat on a mat.

"Don't worry, that is why we are friends," Usoko replied.

"What about the rent, how much are we going to pay?"

"Don't worry about that. When I told her about your problems, she was reasonable and allowed you to occupy the house for free, until you get another one."

"May God reward you and your friend for your kindness."

"Amen!" Usoko replied. "I am sure your problems will be solved. I had better be going. I am expecting a visitor at home."

"Okay, thank you once again."

*

One month later, Gawi's children temporarily withdrew from school because she couldn't afford to pay the fees.

Gawi was alone in the room, busy cleaning her cooking stuff. The children had gone out.

Usoko visited to see how they were doing. She knocked on the door and entered the room.

"You are welcome," Gawi said, as she cleaned her hands with a rag to hug Usoko.

Immediately Usoko sat on the bed, Gawi also sat beside her.

"How are you and the children?"

"We thank God. Except that they have been complaining of hunger."

"Hunger! Don't you have food?"

"Even a single measure of flour is not available," Gawi answered worriedly.

"Why didn't you inform me the last time I came?"

"I was thinking you have done a lot for us that is why I didn't want to bother you again."

"Don't worry about that. As from today, whenever you are in need and you think I can assist, you should not hesitate to tell me."

Gawi nodded.

Usoko opened her bag and removed some money. "Take this four thousand Naira. You can manage with it for a while."

"Thank you very much," Gawi replied, collecting the money.

Usoko was quiet for a short time. "Gawi," she said, as she moved closer in curiosity. "There is a question that I have wanted to ask you, but it has been escaping my mind."

"What question?"

"Where is Twalbani?"

The question was unexpected. It struck Gawi hard. Immediately, the hatred she had for Twalbani resurfaced in her mind. Her facial expression suddenly changed. "When I brought Twalbani to our house, I thought he was good and trustworthy. After a particular event, I knew he wasn't."

"What happened?"

"There was a time I kept ten thousand Naira in my bedroom and went to work. Before I came back, he broke my door and stole the money. Since then I have not set eyes on him. He ran away," Gawi explained.

"How sure are you that he was the person who stole the money?"

"My children saw him when he was breaking the door. I am sure they would not lie to me."

"Why would he do such a thing? That boy looked so innocent. I hope one day he will realize his mistake and come back home," Usoko remarked angrily.

"I have forgiven him. The money is not even as important to me as seeing him."

CHAPTER 6

After a few years, Twalbani graduated from secondary school with a good result. Mwashat was happy with his progress. Twalbani was passionate by God's grace about talking to people on the love of God. He was also committed to overcoming sexual immorality and encouraging others to do so for the glory of God.

Twalbani got admission to a University abroad where he did well. He returned to Nigeria and joined the company of Mwashat. He later fell in love with a girl. They eventually got married even though Mwashat had remained a bachelor.

Mwashat eventually became ill and died. His death was a huge shock to Twalbani and many others. He had willed his possessions to the care of Twalbani. It was a big challenge for Twalbani because some of the late Mwashat's relatives wanted his possessions. They tried hard to fight the contents of the will, but they could not go above the law. The late Mwashat's lawyer insisted that the will must be respected.

Twalbani's previous early experiences with his paternal relatives after the death of his father had taught him some lessons. He knew how selfish and aggressive some people can be over material possessions. He did not let the bitter reactions from the late Mwashat's relatives to bother him much.

Eventually, Twalbani took over the company as the Chief Executive Officer. His leadership style, like Mwashat's, was effective.

*

The area where Gawi lived was looking dirty as usual. Smoke from a fire was also contributing to its pollution that day. Many people were busy with their activities.

Gawi and her children moved from the one room to two rooms in the same compound. Three years ago, she got a job with a small private company. Her salary was small, but enough to buy food and pay the rent for their two rooms. Her son was also working with a company as a casual labourer, but he was not assisting the family properly. Her daughters spent most of their time in beer parlours, where different men took advantage of them.

Gawi sat on her bed in her room as she prepared a trap for the rats that had been disturbing her. Her children were not at home.

In the street leading to Gawi's house, an expensive car was seen. Many people curiously looked at the car. When the car reached a particular point, it stopped. The door opened and Twalbani came out with a sad face, holding a brief case. He walked slowly to Gawi's house. On reaching there, he knocked on the door. Gawi responded and came to meet him. She did not have a clue as to who he was.

Twalbani had earlier hired a private investigator who was able to trace Gawi's house. It was a difficult decision to visit her.

"Good afternoon, Madam," Twalbani greeted her, breaking into her moment of contemplation.

"Good afternoon, sir," she replied nervously. "May I help you?"

"Yes. May I come in?"

"Come in," she invited.

Twalbani walked in. Gawi removed some clothes from the bed for him to sit down.

"Thank you," he said, while sitting down.

Gawi stared at him curiously. There was silence for a short time.

"Are you Mrs. Puranza?"

"Yes, how did you know me?"

"That's not the issue. I want to ask you a question."

"What is that?"

"Do you know where Twalbani is?"

At the mention of Twalbani, Gawi became upset and immediately felt her old inner hatred for him. It showed clearly on her face. She was wondering why the sudden question from a stranger. "Why do you want to know?" Gawi politely asked.

Twalbani smiled at her. "Please, tell me if you know where he is?"

"I don't know where he is now. Since he stole my money some years ago, he ran out of my house," Gawi explained with confidence.

"Stole your money?" Twalbani asked in surprise.

"Yes. He was a thief - that is why he left."

Twalbani kept quiet for a moment. "Madam, you must have at least an idea of where he is now."

Gawi was silent.

Twalbani bowed his head and tears filled his eyes.

"Are you okay?" Gawi asked, standing up.

Twalbani lifted his head and looked at her in tears.

Gawi wondered why he was crying. The situation was confusing her.

"Aunty."

Gawi became even more confused at hearing him call her that.

"I am Twalbani," he disclosed, with more tears rolling down his cheeks.

"What! You are Twalbani?"

Twalbani nodded.

Gawi kept quiet in deep thought.

Twalbani stared at her gently. He was still in tears.

"I hope you are not here to harm me?" Gawi inquired in anxiety and fear.

"Don't be scared. I have already forgiven you by the grace of God."

Gawi started crying. "Please, don't add to my sorrows. I know I am a wicked woman and I don't deserve mercy from you," she lamented, as she knelt down before him. "Forgive me, Twalbani. Forgive me!" she begged earnestly.

"I do not hate you. Jesus taught me to love and forgive those who do wrong to me."

"I am sorry!" Gawi exclaimed repeatedly.

Twalbani turned and took his brief case. "Aunty, I don't like this place you are living in. I have already prepared a better accommodation for you. This is two hundred thousand Naira," he said while leaving the brief case on the bed. "Take care of yourself and the children. I will come back soon, God willing." He walked out of the room to his car still crying.

As he approached the car, Gawi came out weeping, calling his name and running towards him. Twalbani also turned and ran to her. They met and hugged each other, weeping bitterly for some minutes.

CHAPTER 7

"That was how Twalbani and Gawi were reconciled. She and her children relocated to a better house. Twalbani loved them and shared the gospel to them. Eventually, they accepted Jesus as their Lord and Saviour. Gawi's daughters stopped their bad lifestyle. Ndabo got a job at Twalbani's company. Twalbani set up a good business for Gawi and helped her children secure admissions to schools. He sponsored them through different levels and they finished successfully," Nachau concluded his narration.

Ntulo, Yansurili, and Akio looked at Nachau solemnly. The story had really penetrated deep into them. Tears filled up their eyes.

"That is really a thought- provoking story," Ntulo said.

Yansurili nodded in agreement.

Lisami was expectant of the next stage. The story of Twalbani and his aunt also moved her to tears. She pondered whether she could forgive the family of Ntulo like Twalbani did to Gawi. To her his forgiving spirit was strange and extraordinary. She could only wish to be like him from a distance.

Suddenly, choosing between staying with the family of Ntulo and going back to the village crossed her mind. Hunger in the village or maltreatment in the city? She was confused. The memory of her parents was active in her mind. Eventually, she concluded that it was better to remain a slave in the city than die of hunger in the village. Her wish was for Nachau and Akio to prevail on Ntulo and Yansurili to change their attitude towards her.

"You never know who will help you in the journey of life. The person you least expected may turn out to help you have a better living tomorrow. Any kindness you give to someone will one day return to you bigger. Everyone is part of your wider family unit," Nachau emphasized.

Ntulo and Yansurili stared at each other. Their faces showed that they were struggling with the lessons of the story.

Nachau and Akio looked on, hoping for a positive response.

"Most importantly, we need to help people not because we expect help in return, but because of unconditional love," Nachau added.

"Thank you, sir, for challenging us and letting us understand better the value of kindness and forgiveness. We will need some time to discuss. You will know our decision soon by the grace of God," Ntulo stated.

Yansurili nodded in support.

"We will come to your house once we reach a decision," Ntulo said.

Nachau and Akio kept quiet for a while.

"You don't need to come to our house. You can call us once you are ready. It will be a delight for us to come back to your house to hear your decision. We started it here; it is good we finish it here," Nachau commented.

"Okay, sir. We will do just that," Ntulo remarked.

*

Ntulo was uncertain about his position, but Yansurili had already made up her mind.

"I was really touched by the story Nachau shared. I saw myself in the position of Gawi, and Lisami in the position of Twalbani. It is a fact that we need to consider so that we don't end up as victims. We should love Lisami unconditionally so that she can live better as a member of this family," Ntulo said.

Yansurili was quiet for a short time. "I think you are losing your senses. I am really disappointed at your conclusion!"

Ntulo stared at his wife.

"Do you think anything good will come out of Lisami? Maybe you need to look at her again. She does not look like someone who will be useful to us in future. Twalbani was only lucky to have met Mwashat, which was why he succeeded."

"I am not losing my senses. It is what I am feeling as the right thing for us to do. Nachau was right. We don't know the person that will help us tomorrow."

"Are you now trying to allow Nachau to think for us? Does he know our problems? It is better you forget about what he said and think for yourself. He is a man just like you. We should not allow him to interfere with our decision. If he succeeds this time, he will interfere again!" Yansurili reacted angrily.

"Twalbani's story is a reminder of my story. How I suffered while growing up. Based on your story of how you grew up too, it also portrays similar contents. For the first time since Lisami came to our house I felt guilty about how we have been treating her. Our stories should never be wasted. We should use the same comfort and encouragement we got from others to encourage her."

"Enough of this nonsense! Lisami is not part of this family and there is nobody that can change that! She is a liability to us! We cannot afford to keep her here. I don't want to hear anything different from my opinion."

Ntulo was quiet for a moment. "But...."

"We are done with this matter!" Yansurili stood up and left the room.

Ntulo was speechless as he watched his wife leave the room. He also stood up and went out.

*

Two days later, Nachau and Akio were still highly expectant. They had been praying for Ntulo and Yansurili to make the right decision.

Lisami was anxious. She had sleepless nights in contemplation of the outcome.

In the afternoon, Nachau's cell phone rang. He was happy to see Ntulo's name. He invited them to their house for a discussion as agreed. Quickly, Nachau and Akio got ready and walked to the house. They met Ntulo and Yansurili waiting for them in the parlour.

Nachau and Akio were welcomed in and offered some water to drink. The discussion started after the normal greetings.

"We are grateful for your intervention. We know it is because you care that you came. As you already know my wife and I have respect for you. We will go straight to the point about our decision," Ntulo said.

Yansurili nodded.

Lisami was anxiously listening from her room.

"We cannot continue to keep Lisami in our house. She has to return to the village. She is a burden, not a blessing to us. We have lost our interest in keeping her," Ntulo disclosed.

Nachau and Akio were silent.

Ntulo and Yansurili stared at them, ready to defend their position.

"Are you sure that this is what you want to do?" Nachau asked politely.

"With due respect, sir, that is the position of our family," Yansurili answered.

"A question was asked, 'How do you catch a black hen in darkness?'" Nachau asked.

"Light is needed," Ntulo answered after deep thought.

"Similarly, Lisami needs light to find her path in the dark," Nachau explained.

Ntulo and Yansurili kept quiet. Their faces still showed insistence on their decision.

"We would not want to interfere with your family's decision, but remember that a child belongs to everybody. We are guardians of one another," Nachau stated.

"We stand by our decision," Yansurili responded quickly.

Lisami rushed out to the parlour. She knelt down before Yansurili and held her legs, weeping. "Please, Madam, don't take me back to the village. I will suffer from hunger there. I promise to do whatever you want me to do. If I make any mistake, you have the right to beat me however you want to; but please don't send me back to the village. You don't have to even worry about enrolling me in school. I will stay at home and work for you," she pleaded.

Yansurili ignored the pleas and pulled her legs away from Lisami's hands. Lisami fell on the tiled floor and hit her head hard because of the force of the pull. Regardless of that she continued to beg.

Tears rolled down the cheeks of Akio as she looked at the scene.

"Considering Lisami's pleas, do you still want to send her back to the village?" Nachau focused on Ntulo as he inquired earnestly.

"Yes, we do!" Yansurili answered harshly.

Ntulo looked on. In his heart he was worried, but did not want to oppose his wife.

"When do you want to return her?" Akio asked.

"Tomorrow," Yansurili quickly replied.

"What time?" Akio inquired.

"At 10 am," Yansurili remarked.

Nachau and his wife looked at each other. Their facial expressions showed that they had made a decision. "We will come to the house at

9:30 am, God willing, and go to the village with you. We would love to have Lisami in our family," Nachau announced.

Ntulo and Yansurili looked at each other.

"That will not be a problem if Lisami and her aunt agree," Yansurili stated.

The news came to Lisami as a surprise. She sensed that the intention of Nachau and Akio was the best way out of her problems. As far as she was concerned, they did not have to ask for her opinion. It was complete approval from her.

After some further discussion, Nachau and Akio went back home.

CHAPTER 8

Nachau and others went to Lisami's village to discuss with the aunt. Nachau and Akio seriously thought about the difficulties Kunpira might have in releasing Lisami considering the maltreatment in Ntulo's house.

Kunpira was working on a farm close to their compound when Nachau and others reached the village. One of her children went and informed her about the arrival of the guests. Her husband had gone out to visit a friend.

The guests were already seated on wooden chairs when Kunpira came. She became curious when she saw Lisami holding her bag among them. Yansurili had earlier called and informed her of their visit, but did not mention coming with Lisami. Seeing Nachau and Akio whom she had never met raised fear in her mind. "Maybe Lisami has done something wrong," she reasoned within herself. "You are all welcome," Kunpira said while placing her hoe by the door of her hut.

The guests responded.

Kunpira went and washed her hands. She asked one of her children to bring drinking water for the guests.

She joined them after a moment and expected Ntulo or Yansurili to speak. Her curiosity did not allow her to go into further greetings or wait for Nachau and Akio to be introduced to her.

"You did not mention coming with Lisami. I hope there is no problem?" she asked anxiously.

Ntulo stared at his wife, expecting her to speak first, but Yansurili signalled with her hand for him to take the lead.

Ntulo cleared his throat and waited again in silence. Kunpira needed him to speak quickly to release her of her confusion.

"We are here to return Lisami to you," Ntulo informed.

Kunpira looked at Ntulo keenly and turned to Lisami who was already crying.

"Why? Has she done something wrong?" Kunpira inquired.

Ntulo looked at his wife expecting her to give the explanation. "Yes. We felt we cannot continue to keep her in our house," he said when he realized that his wife was not willing to fully participate.

"What have you done wrong?" Kunpira asked Lisami quickly.

Lisami was still crying.

"You better answer my question. Don't waste my time with your tears!" Kunpira shouted.

Lisami still could not reply as expected.

"Speak so that I can beg Mr. and Mrs. Ntulo on your behalf!"

"I don't know what I have done that made them bring me back. They can explain to you," Lisami replied calmly.

Nachau and Akio watched and listened.

"Her explanation is not important at this point. Since we took her to the city from you, it is proper we bring her back when we feel she cannot continue living with us," Yansurili mentioned.

"I am still in the dark. I need to know what she did to help me know how to talk to her," Kunpira remarked.

"She is lazy, stubborn and stole from us," Yansurili said.

"It is not true!" Lisami reacted.

"Shut up! I hope you have not forgotten that it is a mark of disrespect to respond to an elder that way!" Kunpira shouted at Lisami.

"But what she said is not true," Lisami affirmed.

"Let me not hear you say that again!" Kunpira responded.

Lisami kept quiet.

"Please, forgive her. Sometimes children can easily miss the road," Kunpira stated.

"That is okay," Yansurili said.

Nachau wanted to intervene, but he needed to understand the situation before any active involvement.

"We want you to accept her back knowing full well that we have tried our best," Ntulo emphasized.

"She is only a child. You don't have to bring her back. With little patience I am sure she would become better. We are suffering in this village. Bringing her back will not help her or us. It will affect her education since we don't have a good school here," Kunpira explained.

"I have not been enrolled in school since I left the village!" Lisami reported.

"Keep quiet and allow me to beg Mr. and Mrs. Ntulo!" Kunpira rebuked.

"I am telling you the truth," Lisami insisted.

Kunpira kept quiet and turned to Yansurili. "Is it true that you did not enrol her in school?" she asked anxiously.

Yansurili did not talk.

"Please, tell me it is not true," Kunpira said, as she turned to Ntulo. "Your silence is an indication that Lisami was right."

"That is not why we are here," Yansurili replied. "It is time for us to go."

Kunpira jumped to her feet angrily. "I won't let you go until you answer my question."

Ntulo and Yansurili stared at Kunpira. They knew she was serious considering her readiness for further action.

Nachau and Akio were anxious for their turn to speak.

"We could not enrol her because of her attitude," Ntulo answered.

"You people are wicked!" Kunpira said while turning to Yansurili. "Last year, you told me that Lisami was doing well in school?" she added furiously.

Yansurili stared at her.

"You have betrayed our trust. You have also cheated this girl even when you know that enrolling her in school was the main reason I let her go with you to the city!"

"You can say whatever you want. We have not cheated anybody. Lisami is back to you and that is all that matters to us!" Yansurili reacted. "These people," pointing at Nachau and Akio, "are here to talk to you. They want to continue from where we stopped."

"I am not afraid of you. Just because you have money does not give you the right to maltreat us!" Kunpira reacted angrily.

"Let us go," Yansurili said to her husband. They stood up and went to the car.

Kunpira shouted at them. Some people came around when they heard her.

Ntulo quickly started the car and drove away.

After an hour, calmness was restored. Kunpira sat down deep in thought.

"Sometimes things do not go according to our plans," Nachau interrupted Kunpira's moment of silence. "I am Nachau and my wife is Akio." He further introduced themselves to Kunpira.

Kunpira stared at them as she listened.

"Considering what had happened this might not be the best moment to talk to you in detail about our intention, but it is good we mention it," Nachau said.

Lisami's attention was on her aunt.

"We met with Lisami in one of her terrible moments. We tried to persuade Mr. and Mrs. Ntulo to change their way of relating to her. After due consideration, we decided to have Lisami in our family, God willing," Nachau explained.

Kunpira looked at Nachau and Akio angrily.

"We promise you that Lisami will be treated well by the grace of God. We need your approval," Nachau affirmed.

Kunpira behaved as if she did not hear what Nachau had said. "Lisami," Kunpira called.

"Yes," Lisami quickly answered.

"Take your bag into the hut you occupied before you left for the city."

Lisami was reluctant.

"Take your bag to the hut!" Kunpira shouted in anger.

Lisami took the bag and walked slowly to the hut.

"I will never trust anybody from the city again," Kunpira said.

Lisami was eager to know the outcome of the discussion.

"We know it is not easy for you. You are hurting right now, but you will not know us better until you give us the chance to assist," Nachau remarked.

"Please, do not waste your time. I will never change my mind."

"Fire can destroy," Nachau stated. "It can also produce good things. So are human beings. You have experienced the negative side; give us a chance to try showing the other side. We would not betray you, by God's grace."

"You cannot change my mind on this matter," Kunpira replied.

Akio wanted to talk, but Nachau signalled her not to.

"Thank you for your time. We need to be on our way. We hope that your mind will be fruitful on this matter when we meet again," Nachau stated.

Akio did not understand why Nachau did not persist. Lisami too was in confusion. She ran out of the hut and hugged Akio in tears.

Kunpira stood up and pulled Lisami off Akio. "You will know the extent of my anger if you don't go back to your hut, now!" Kunpira reacted. "Please, leave my house," she said to Nachau and Akio.

Nachau and Akio entered their car and drove away, leaving Lisami in the village, but at the same time travelling with her in their hearts.

"I thought you would persist," Akio said.

"Sometimes withdrawal is another way of building persistence. Her heart was injured. She would understand us better another time," Nachau replied.

At night, Lisami spent almost an hour crying. She deeply wondered about her future in the village.

Later, when Kunpira's husband returned and saw Lisami, and been informed of what had happened, he reluctantly welcomed her back.

*

The next morning, around 6 am, Lisami was awakened for the farm. They worked for about three hours before breakfast was served. They sat under a tree and ate. After that, they worked till late afternoon before they went back home.

Lisami thought carefully on the potential kindness of Nachau's family. Her body ached when she went to sleep at night because of the hard physical work on the farm. Before leaving the village, she had never been involved in such farming.

The same farming routine continued the next day. They finished their work earlier and went home.

Later in the evening, Lisami went out of the house and sat on a stone thinking. An old man, named Zali, the richest man in the village passed her on his motorcycle. He turned back to her when he saw her. He was seventy-five years old. He and his wife had ten children. Most of his children were married and living in the village.

"What is your name?" Zali asked when he stopped before her.

Lisami was quiet looking at him.

"Don't be afraid. Tell me your name."

"Lisami," she replied reluctantly.

"From where did you come from?"

"The house of Chambasom," she answered while pointing at the house.

"Are you the daughter of late Kurum?"

"Yes."

"You have really grown up. I am told that you returned from the city. "

Lisami nodded.

"What are you doing here alone?"

Lisami looked at him in silence.

"Take this money and buy yourself something good to eat," he said as he removed the money from one of the pockets of his trouser. "Stop wasting time here. Your father was a good friend to one of my sons," he added.

"I don't need it. I am thinking of something else."

Zali insisted, but Lisami refused to collect the money. He rode back to his house thinking of her.

*

The next day, early in the morning, Zali came to Chambasom's house and asked him for a discussion. Chambasom and his wife were surprised and curious at Zali's visit. He was known as a proud person who doesn't visit those he considered poor.

Zali and Chambasom went outside the house and sat on a log of wood.

"You may be wondering the reason for this visit," Zali said.

"Yes, being your first time," Chambasom remarked.

"Never mind. Today is the right time for the visit."

"What can I do for you, sir?"

"I am aware that you have been thinking of having a better living?"

"Yes," Chambasom answered quickly.

"I also know that your wife needed a big land to expand her farm this season."

"Yes, sir."

"All these are possible. I can give you money and make you one of my farm managers. I can also give your wife a big land and improved variety of seedlings for her farm."

"Thank you for your kind considerations," Chambasom said happily.

Zali smiled

"But to what do we owe these favours?"

Zali kept quiet for a while. "I want to have Lisami as my wife," he stated with a little pride.

Chambasom was speechless.

"I know you will not reject my request."

"That is not for me to decide alone. I will discuss with my wife and let you know of the outcome," Chambasom replied slowly.

"I know she is the one that can formally respond to my request since the girl is related to her. I also know that a man can influence his wife in decision making."

"I will try my best."

"Take this money for your outing today. A man needs money in his pocket to remain a man." Zali gave Chambasom some amount of money.

"Thank you for this wonderful gift. You have made my day," Chambasom responded with a smile.

"I am counting on you for success."

"Don't worry. Money can do what words cannot do. My wife will reason with me when she sees the money."

Zali removed some amount of money and gave to Chambasom. "This is for your wife."

"This is too much. You are already successful," Chambasom assured.

*

Lisami was sitting outside their house when suddenly she saw an emaciated girl with firewood on her head and a baby on her back. Her shirt was torn and her baby's hair brownish. On a closer look, she identified her as Dikyam, her childhood friend.

Lisami called.

Dikyam stopped reluctantly.

Lisami hurriedly walked to her.

"Lisami, you are welcome back," Dikyam said.

"Thank you. How are you?"

"I am not doing good."

"What happened? You look different," Lisami curiously asked.

"Em … My friend, I am struggling with various challenges. I learnt of your return, but I am too ashamed to meet you the way I am."

"Whose baby is this," Lisami asked, pointing at the baby.

"Mine. That is one of the reasons I said I am struggling with various challenges."

"Are you married?"

"Please, Lisami, don't torture me with questions. I am not married. My sorrows control me. This village favours those that are eager to destroy themselves."

Lisami listened.

"After I became pregnant, the man abandoned me to my parents. He left the village to the city. I still have not heard from him."

"What about his parents?"

"They are here, but they too are suffering. They cannot remember me in their misery."

"I also have various challenges."

"I felt sad when I heard of your return. Many things have changed in this village. Find a way of leaving quickly or else darkness will soon become your closest friend."

"You now speak like an adult," Lisami said.

"I have learnt some lessons from my challenges."

"How are our other friends?"

"They are also struggling. I know where you can meet them, but you will enjoy their company only when you are willing to do what they do."

"What is that?"

"I will take you if you no longer have any good plan for the future."

"I will think about it."

The two friends discussed other things. Lisami watched Dikyam as she walked away, until she got out of sight.

*

Kunpira invited Lisami for a discussion at night. They sat on stools in the middle of the compound. Kunpira placed a local lantern on the ground. Some insects came out of the darkness and flew around it.

"I am worried about your return to this village. Young girls hardly survive pregnancy outside of marriage. I don't want you to end up like Dikyam, your friend. Did you meet her since your return?

"Yes. We met today."

"Were you happy with what you saw?"

"I really felt bad."

"You may end up like her if you are not careful."

"I don't want to end up like that."

"What do you think you can do to avoid it?"

"I still feel that Mr. and Mrs. Nachau would not fail like Mr. and Mrs. Ntulo. Please, let me live with them."

"That will never happen! It is better you forget about that. I have my plan for you."

"Kindly allow me to pursue my passion for schooling in the city."

"My plan for you is better."

Lisami kept quiet.

"Do you know Zali, the richest man in the village?"

Lisami stared at Kunpira anxiously.

"Answer the question. Don't stare at me like that."

"Yes," Lisami answered reluctantly.

"He wants your hand in marriage."

Lisami felt like she was having a dream, and needed someone to wake her up from sleep.

"He is also willing to make us rich if you marry him."

"Please, don't do this to me. My sorrows are already too much for me to bear," Lisami calmly remarked.

"You must marry him!"

"If you force me, you will give me no choice, but to run away to Mr. and Mrs. Nachau."

"You must do as I said!"

"I plead with you, Aunty. I need to go to school. Allow me to live with Mr. and Mrs. Nachau," Lisami begged, while holding on to Kunpira's leg.

"Think about my plan, and let me know your decision in the morning," Kunpira responded, as she pulled her legs away from Lisami's hands. She stood up and walked into her hut.

For more than two hours Lisami sat alone outside contemplating the situations. Mosquitoes feasted on her. Hatred for Ntulo and Yansurili resurfaced strongly in her. She wished she had control over their lives. Her vengeance would surely make them feel pains. She wept bitterly and looked up to the sky. All she could see were dark clouds, the moon and stars.

"God, please, help me. I am confused and frustrated. I feel like killing myself. Send help to me just like you did to Twalbani. Touch my aunt's heart to support my plan. In Jesus' name I prayed. Amen."

She was quiet after the prayer. After some time, she stood up and entered her hut.

*

Early in the morning, Kunpira called Lisami twice, but she did not answer. She entered her hut, but there was nobody there. She went out and shouted her name again.

Chambasom came out and asked the reason for the shouting.

"Lisami is not in her room," Kunpira said.

"Maybe she has gone to the river to fetch some water."

"We have enough water in the house. She had earlier threatened to run away to Mr. and Mrs. Nachau if I force her to marry Zali," Kunpira explained.

"We should first search for her in the village. You should go and ask Dikyam," Chambasom suggested.

"Okay." Kunpira went to Dikyam's house, but Lisami was not there. She returned and informed Chambasom.

Chambason advised that they should wait for two hours, maybe she would return. After two hours, Lisami has not yet returned. Chambason invited some young men and asked for their help in searching for Lisami in the forest.

Nachau and Akio were restless. They felt a strong need to go to the village and continue discussion with Kunpira. They arrived at the village after Chambason and the youth have gone to the forest.

Kunpira was surprised, but happy to see them. She ran to them as they came out of the vehicle. "Have you seen Lisami?" she inquired anxiously.

"No. What happened?" Akio asked quickly.

"She is missing. She had earlier threatened to run away to you people," Kunpira explained.

"Calm down. God willing, she will be found," Akio assured. "We need to be hopeful and keep on searching. She might still be in the village," she added.

"Where is your husband?" Nachau asked.

"He has gone with some young men to the forest in search of her," Kunpira responded.

"Let us wait for their return," Nachau stated. "It is important we pray," he added.

Nachau led the prayer session for some minutes. After that they found chairs and sat down.

Chambasom and the youth were careful in the search. They even climbed the mountains. After about three hours, one of them saw a young girl under a tree lying on the ground. When he went there, he saw Lisami sleeping. He called her name and she woke up in fear. She immediately attempted to run away. He sounded an alarm and the rest came to his direction. Chambason held her tightly and dragged her, but she tried to resist.

"I will not go back!" Lisami shouted.

"You have no choice!" Chambason reacted.

One of the muscular young men lifted her up, put her on his shoulder and walked home as she struggled to free herself.

Kunpira, Nachau and Akio were happy when they saw the team returning with Lisami. Immediately they arrived, the young man dropped her on the ground.

Kunpira slapped her out of anger and beat her with a cane. "Your stubbornness has caused us pains!" she said angrily.

"This is a time for joy, not for anger. Let us not add to her sorrows," Nachau advised.

Lisami stood up, ran and hugged Akio. "Please, don't let them force me into marriage. I want to go to school in the city. Help me!" Lisami begged in tears.

"We are here for you. We trust God will give us the favour we need. Stop crying and be strong," Akio encouraged.

"Come here!" Kunpira shouted.

Still crying, Lisami held Akio tightly. "Help me!" she begged.

Nachau and Akio pleaded with Kunpira to handle her gently. It took some minutes before Kunpira was persuaded.

Chambason thanked the young men and let them go.

The discussions over Lisami living with Nachau's family lasted for more than an hour. To confirm their commitment to the well-being of Lisami, Nachau told Kunpira and Chambason to visit them after three months of Lisami living with them. They reserve the right to take her away if there is not any improvement in her development.

Kunpira and Chambasom finally agreed to let Lisami live with Nachau's family. They were convinced Lisami would run away again if they forced her to marry Zali.

Chambasom asked to see his wife in the hut.

"What do we tell Zali?" Chambasom asked when they entered the hut.

"We would tell him the truth."

"What about his money?" Chambasom inquired anxiously.

"Did we ask him to give us? We would know what to tell him when he comes."

Nachau, Akio and Lisami eventually left the village in happiness. The journey back to the city for Lisami was like walking out of a lion's mouth into freedom.

CHAPTER 9

Lisami was warmly welcomed by Nachau's family members. Ndatam, Nachau's daughter, quickly showed Lisami her room. It was well furnished and neat. Everything in the room made her understand that she was truly home.

Lisami was more relaxed with Ndatam than Mijah, Nachau's son. Her past experience with Gandiban at the Ntulo's house was still strong on her mind. She felt Mijah could also abuse her.

At night, Nachau sent Mijah to call Lisami. She was in the room when Mijah knocked on the door. She kept quiet after the first and second knocks.

"Who is it?" she asked fearfully after the third knock.

"Mijah."

"Please, go away. I will not open the door!"

"Why?" Mijah asked curiously.

Lisami was silent for a while. "Please, go away. I beg you. I don't want you to come in," she stated.

"Daddy wants to talk with you."

"I don't believe you."

"What is wrong?" Mijah inquired anxiously.

Lisami was silent.

Mijah eventually got tired of talking to Lisami. He went and informed his father about the situation. Nachau went with him and knocked.

"Lisami. Please, open the door," Nachau said.

Lisami calmed down when she heard the voice of Nachau and opened the door.

Mijah frowned a bit, but Nachau smiled.

"Why did you refuse to open the door?" Mijah asked.

"I don't want what happened to me at Ntulo's house to repeat itself here," Lisami remarked slowly after a moment of silence.

"What happened?" Mijah inquired quickly.

"I don't want to talk about it," Lisami responded.

"That's okay. Let us go to the parlour," Nachau interrupted.

Nachau knew that care was needed if they were going to help Lisami come to terms with who she was, and what had happened to her.

Mijah went to his room, while Nachau and Lisami went to the parlour. Lisami sat on the tiled floor in expectation.

"Please, sit on the chair," Nachau said.

That came to Lisami as a surprise. Throughout her stay at the Ntulo's house, she had never been allowed to sit on any of the chairs in the parlour. Only the parents, children and their guests were allowed to use them.

"I am comfortable here."

"You are a member of this family. You have the right to enjoy the house the way any of us does," Nachau remarked.

Lisami nodded. She stood up and sat on a chair.

"That's better," Nachau stated.

Lisami was still not comfortable.

"I want us to talk."

"Okay, sir."

"You don't need to call me sir. You are not a house girl here, but our daughter. Feel free to call me Daddy, and my wife Mummy. My son, Mijah, and daughter, Ndatam, are your brother and sister respectively."

Lisami nodded again in silence.

"I am aware that various bad things have happened to you. You might be thinking, apart from your parents, no one cares for you."

Lisami looked at Nachau calmly.

"Whatever negative thoughts you have about yourself and other people are all the result of your experiences. Tonight, I want you to start looking at your journey of life differently."

Lisami listened carefully.

"How could you describe your journey after the death of your parents?"

Lisami thought deeply.

Nachau waited patiently for her to respond when suddenly she burst into tears. He did not tell her to stop because he knew that the process was necessary to help her unburden herself.

"Many people are wicked. Sometimes I feel like killing myself. I don't know why I came into this world. Many of those who were close to my parents when they were alive forsook me after their death. When Ntulo and Yansurili came, I thought they would help me; but they were the worst. Some of the things I experienced in their house are too shameful to talk about."

"Sharing your experiences with me will help us find better ways of supporting you."

"I cannot share some of them. It is better I don't talk about them!"

"That is okay. I hope that one day you will have the strength to talk about them."

"This world is not for people like me. I can never be somebody important!" she said, as she wept more.

Nachau waited for her to finish weeping. "It is time for you to wake up from sorrow and start living better. You need to learn some important lessons from your experiences."

Lisami listened thoughtfully.

"Hot water is afraid of time because it can change its condition. You are hot now, but it is just a matter of time. You will recover."

Lisami went on listening.

"Freedom is not problem-free living, but problem-solving living. There is nobody that is useless. God loves you so much and He wants you to realize that. If you are not seen as special by some people, you are special to God. You were created for His purpose. He will use you to bless this generation and beyond."

Lisami stared at Nachau. She started crying again. Nobody had ever spoken to her like that. Nachau's words were encouraging. She had never known how special she was to God. Neither her parents, nor Kunpira and Chambasom had told her. Ntulo and Yansurili had mentioned the love of God during devotions, but she could not understand it because of their attitude towards her.

"Ntulo and Yansurili are not your enemies. You should learn to forgive them."

"I can't forgive them, Daddy!" Lisami quickly said angrily still in tears. "They don't deserve it."

"You will injure yourself the more if you refuse to forgive. Don't let their attitude to you to harm yours. You will never enjoy living until you have first experienced being a forgiver. Forgivers think better, act better and enjoy special peace in their hearts that leads them to creativity."

Lisami stopped crying and was quiet for a while. "It is not easy to do that. The story of Twalbani you shared has really challenged me. I overheard it from my room."

"It is great to know that. Twalbani forgave Gawi only by the grace of God. It takes love to do what is abnormal. None of us can live well in isolation. We need forgiveness to co-exist efficiently."

Lisami looked at Nachau silently.

"Have you ever made a commitment to serve Jesus?"

"No," she replied.

Nachau explained to Lisami the truth about salvation in Jesus. She eventually understood and accepted Jesus as Lord and Saviour. That night, Lisami knew the greatest peace she had ever known.

The next day, after devotion, Mijah called Lisami aside.

"My sister, I don't know the whole story of what you went through in the house of Ntulo and Yansurili. I want you to know that I will not cheat you. I will relate to you as I do to Ndatam. Please, don't be scared of me again. We are a family. You are safe here by the grace of God," Mijah said.

Lisami was silent.

"We should support each other in our development. God will never let us down."

Lisami nodded.

*

On Sunday, Nachau and his family went to the Church. People greeted each other after the service. Nachau and Akio were busy shaking hands and wishing people well. Mijah, Ndatam and Lisami were close to them. A few of Mijah and Ndatam's friends also came by and greeted.

Lisami was anxiously waiting for them to finish. Suddenly, Ntulo and Yansurili came to Nachau and Akio. Lisami was sad when she saw them. She felt like having the authority to put them in prison for many years over what they did to her. Hatred towards them was dominating her thoughts.

"Good morning, Mr. Nachau," Ntulo greeted.

"Morning, Mr. Ntulo. How is the family?" Nachau inquired.

"Everyone is doing fine," Ntulo answered.

Yansurili also greeted.

Nachau and Akio responded to her.

Lisami wondered why Nachau and Akio were nice to Ntulo and his wife. She wished they would be hard on them so that they would regret their actions to her. Surprisingly, she saw Yansurili walking towards her.

"How are you Lisami?" Yansurili asked politely.

Lisami looked at her angrily and thought of abusing her or walking away, but she remembered what Nachau had told her that they were not her enemies.

"I am still waiting for your reply," Yansurili said.

"I am fine," Lisami replied faintly.

Yansurili smiled. "That is great," she stated. "We need to be on our way home," she informed Nachau and Akio.

"Okay. Wishing you a wonderful week," Nachau remarked.

"Wishing you the same," Ntulo said.

Akio got involved in a discussion with Lisami on their way home.

"I know it was not easy for you to accept Ntulo's family. Your response to Yansurili was a good part of your healing process" Akio stated.

"I honestly thought of abusing her or walking away. I was surprised at my ability to respond the way I did," Lisami said.

"God's grace is sufficient for us to do what is humanly hard or impossible. You will never have peace if you have bitterness towards Ntulo's family," Akio further encouraged.

"She only pretended to like me. I am sure they still hate me. They are not happy that I am living with you. After discussing with Daddy on forgiveness, I thought I have overcome the bitterness. The reality today was a big test to me. I cannot explain what came over me when I saw them," Lisami explained.

"Maturity is a process. Approach your challenges as a learner by God's grace," Akio commented.

Lisami nodded.

Nachau, Mijah and Ndatam listened attentively.

*

Ntulo and Yansurili were restless because of Lisami's response. They did not discuss the issue on their way back because they were with their children. When they got home, Yansurili went into the bedroom and sat down on the bed. Her mood was low.

Ntulo was in the parlour for some minutes expecting his wife, but she did not show up. He went into the bedroom.

"What is wrong?" Ntulo inquired as he sat down beside her.

Yansurili was quiet.

Ntulo waited for her to speak.

"I only pretended to be happy since we took Lisami back to the village. I have been struggling with guilt," Yansurili said.

Ntulo listened carefully.

"Seeing her today was a reminder of my attitude towards her. I honestly thought she would not answer my question when I greeted her. I was surprised she did despite her struggles. It was one of my most miserable days. God has given her another family. Have you noticed her dress? She was looking beautiful in it. We had our opportunity, but we failed."

Ntulo took a deep breath.

"How I wish we can turn around the time and start afresh."

"You are not the only one struggling with guilt. I tried to forget about it, but I could not. I earlier thought of discussing it with you, but I kept it to myself. I didn't know how you would react. Any time I thought of her or see a girl of her age, I asked myself what of if she was our biological daughter? Or someone does what we did to her to our daughter? She is an orphan who needed our support, but we were not there for her," Ntulo lamented.

"I will not forget Nachau's story of Twalbani and his aunt. The lessons in the story are disturbing me," Yansurili said with tears in her eyes.

Ntulo was silent for awhile.

"What do we do now?" Yansurili asked.

"We should genuinely ask God for forgiveness. We also need to apologize to Lisami. We cannot change what happened, but we can co-support her with Nachau's family," Ntulo suggested.

"We can ask God for forgiveness. However, apologizing to Lisami will not be easy. What will happen if she refuses to accept our apology? Now is not the best time for that. Let us think again, maybe we will have another option. Lisami is only a child. We should not embarrass ourselves," she remarked.

"The embarrassment will not be as frustrating as the guilt we have. We have a choice to make it right or continue to suffer with guilt," Ntulo emphasized.

"Both are challenges. We need to carefully think through our options. Let us not allow guilt to make us do what we would later regret," Yansurili emphasized.

Ntulo kept quiet.

CHAPTER 10

Lisami started school at the primary level. She found it difficult to fit into the system because she felt inferior. She preferred keeping to herself to having friends in school. Some of the girls laughed at her. It was not easy for her to handle the pressure.

One morning, Akio entered Lisami's room to ensure she was ready for school because she did not see her preparing as usual. To her surprise, she found her in bed crying. Akio went and sat beside her.

"Lisami, what is wrong with you?"

Lisami continued to cry.

"Are you not going to school today?"

"I will not go back to school because some girls laughed at me. Yesterday they called me a village girl who cannot do anything good!"

"It is really a challenge, but you cannot solve the problem by crying and complaining like that. It is true that you came from a village, but is there anybody who does not have a beginning from somewhere? Some people started worse than you, but today their stories have changed for good," Akio said.

Lisami listened.

"You are a talented person. It is not true that you cannot do anything good. Those girls did not create you. How would they know that? God knows you as a special person. You need to trust Him."

Lisami continued to listen.

"Last week I asked your teacher how you were doing. She has also noticed your potential intelligence. This is your moment to live better."

"Thank you, Mummy," Lisami remarked politely.

Akio smiled.

"My main problem in learning is how to read well."

"I know. Together we shall solve the problem by God's grace."

"Let me get ready for school."

"Problems should move us forward, not backward," Akio said with a smile.

*

Later in the evening, Nachau invited Lisami to his study. She was eager to talk to him.

"Good evening, Daddy," Lisami greeted, when she entered the study.

"Good evening, my dear. Have a seat."

Lisami sat down.

"How was school today?"

"It was good."

"What made it good? Your mother has told me of your challenges."

"It was good, not because the other girls have stopped bothering me, but because I am a changed girl. After the last discussion with Mummy, I realized that I don't have to allow them frustrate me any longer."

"That is good."

Lisami smiled.

"I need to teach you something important in achieving effective progress."

Lisami sat comfortably to listen.

"There are different forms of courage. Soldiers are courageous in the battlefield. Some are courageous in school as teachers and students. Others in hospitals and other places. One of the great forms of courage is becoming a forgiver. A person who can forgive those who offended him or her is indeed courageous. All of us are alive because of God's forgiveness. There will be people who will offend us. Therefore, we need forgiveness to oil our choices."

"Daddy, I still think it is not easy to do that."

Nachau smiled. "We can do it by God's grace," he affirmed.

Lisami listened carefully.

"There is someone's growth in forgiveness. Someone said, 'When you forgive, you will later discover that the real prisoner you have set free is yourself.'"

"I have never seen life in the way you are helping me to see it. I am truly grateful, Daddy."

"To God be the glory. Keep on trusting Jesus and you will understand the meaning of life better. Let me also share with you some tips that can help you improve your performance in school."

Lisami nodded.

"You don't have to be a good reader before you can read your books. Daily practice is another way of making important progress. It has been suggested that 'reading books improves reading.' It helps you to discover new words. You should check the dictionary for the meanings of the new words as you read. You can feel free to ask your mother or me for guidance in the process. We would make sure we choose good books for you to start reading."

"Okay."

"In school, after every class, you should immediately go through your notes. Don't wait until there is a test or an exam. You will understand your notes better when they are familiar to you than when you apply an emergency approach to them. Reading under test or exam tension does not often guarantee genuine understanding. Students who study only for tests or exams can easily forget key points after the tests or exams."

Lisami listened thoughtfully.

"Try to learn from your classmates who have good values and academically are doing better than you. Their level of commitment can influence yours. Bad company can affect your performance. I also know that there are some teachers who maltreat their students. It is common for students to hate such teachers."

"Like our mathematics teacher. Many students don't like him. He likes beating us in class," Lisami remarked.

Nachau smiled. "When I was your age, I failed mathematics because I did not like the teacher. It has been said that 'You can easily fail the subject of a teacher you don't like.' Avoid the temptation of hating any of your teachers. Always meet them personally for any topic you don't understand. It is very helpful in improving your understanding."

"That is good," Lisami said in excitement.

"Applying a good idea is better than talking about it."

Lisami smiled. "Thank you, Daddy. I am happy to be part of this family."

"We are also happy having you."

CHAPTER 11

Some years later, Lisami's school work had improved considerably. She was a delight to Nachau's family. After primary level, she went to a secondary school and obtained a good result on completion of her studies.

Meanwhile, Gandiban, Ntulo and Yansurili's youngest son became a drug addict, stealing money from his parents to sustain his addiction. Yansurili herself became ill, and was hospitalized. Both of her kidneys failed. She was in need of a healthy kidney. A donation was urgently needed for a kidney transplant. Ntulo offered to donate one of his kidneys, but he was not healthy enough. Their children, after being informed of the risks, refused to be tested. None of them was bold enough to help. Some of Yansurili's relatives were also invited and tested. Two of them were found healthy and suitable to donate, but they later refused to be persuaded. They were afraid, in spite of the doctor's assurances.

Dealing with the problem cost the family a lot of money. In order to raise the funds needed they sold some of their valuable possessions. They also received assistance from some friends and relatives. Nachau's family also supported them.

The first time Lisami heard of Yansurili's health challenges was during their family devotion when Nachau made the announcement and they prayed for her healing.

Later, a bad wish for Yansurili crossed Lisami's mind. She wished the right donor would never be found, so that Yansurili would continue to suffer. However, she quickly dismissed the thought. The story of Twalbani and Gawi kept echoing in her mind.

Ntulo was desperate to support his wife. Announcements were made over the radio, television and newspapers with a compensation of two million Naira to any suitable donor. Two people came for testing, but none of them was healthy enough for the donation. The family members of Ntulo became more desperate and frustrated.

Lisami's concern for Yansurili became high. She tried to get over it, but she couldn't. The more she tried, the more she felt concerned. Eventually, she had a strong desire to visit Yansurili at the hospital and probably be tested. When she shared her concern with Nachau and Akio, they did not stop her, but were worried about the risks if she was found suitable.

The family members of Ntulo were surprised to see Lisami at the hospital visiting Yansurili. They concluded that the reward was her motivation, just like other people. She greeted them, and asked about the condition of Yansurili. Ntulo answered her nervously.

Lisami asked for the doctor's office and Ntulo directed her. Eventually, the test was done and Lisami was found suitable to make the donation.

There was no celebration after the discovery because the Ntulo family members were not sure Lisami would agree to donate. Lisami went back home and informed Nachau and Akio about the result of the test.

"What do you want to do?" Nachau asked anxiously.

"I am confused. I need to really think deeply about it," Lisami answered.

"I have a disturbing feeling about this situation," Akio said.

"As you think over what to do, it is important we meet the doctor in charge of the surgery, and seek for his honest medical advice. Understanding the risks helps in making the right decision," Nachau advised.

They later went to the doctor. He was a consultant with an excellent track record of successful kidney transplants. He explained the risks involved, but assured them that his team would do their best. He confirmed that if the surgery was not done soon, Yansurili would probably die. That announcement came as a huge burden to Lisami.

When they went back home, the concern to donate her kidney to Yansurili was stronger on her. She tried to be free from it, but could not. Eventually she informed Nachau and Akio of her decision to donate the kidney.

Nachau and Akio were worried about Lisami's decision. At night, they went to her room and found her praying and crying. She stopped crying after the prayer and welcomed them. They sat on the bed beside her, Nachau on the right, and Akio on the left.

"Our daughter, we want to talk and pray with you about your decision," Akio said.

"Okay, Mummy," Lisami replied.

"Are you sure you want to do this?" Akio inquired.

Lisami was silent for a while. "It is not an easy decision to make, but I am sure it is the right thing for me to do," she remarked softly.

"I hope it is not about the reward?" Akio asked.

"I don't really know what I want for now."

"We just want to be sure you have the right reason for doing it," Akio stated.

Lisami's facial expression showed the struggles in her.

"Every day of our lives, we have the privilege to serve. If this is how you are convinced to support Yansurili, then let the perfect will of God be done. Our concerns are simply because we are your parents. Doing a good thing with a good motive is a worthy cause," Nachau explained.

Lisami nodded thoughtfully.

"It is important we informed your aunt about your decision. God willing, we will travel to the village tomorrow," Nachau said.

"Okay," Lisami remarked.

After much discussion, they prayed together and left Lisami to sleep.

Akio and Nachau entered their room worriedly. Akio sat on the bed and cried. Nachau sat down beside her. He also felt like crying. He wished a miracle of healing will happen to Yansurili to avoid the kidney donation.

"I am afraid. I don't want us to lose her," Akio stated in tears.

"Crying will not solve the problem. We need to be hopeful that things will go right," Nachau said. "Let us pray," he added.

Akio sobbed as they prayed.

*

At 9 am, the next day, Nachau, Akio and Lisami went to the village and informed Kunpira. Chambasom was not at home.

Kunpira did not want Lisami to take the risk, especially for Yansurili.

Lisami, in compassion, insisted on supporting Yansurili.

"Will they pay for the donation?" Kunpira asked.

Lisami was silent.

Kunpira turned to Nachau and Akio. They also did not answer her question.

"They promised the sum of two million Naira," Lisami answered.

"Two million Naira!" Kunpira shouted in excitement. "You have my permission to give it. Maybe this is the time we have been waiting for."

"It is not right to focus on the money more than Lisami's well-being," Akio quickly said.

"The money is too big to be ignored. We hope the surgery will be successful," Kunpira remarked. "My husband and I will join you tomorrow in the city. We need to support Lisami"

After the meeting, Nachau, Akio and Lisami went back home.

Kunpira later discussed the issue with Chambasom. At first, he was not in support, but he also changed his mind because of the money involved.

*

Kunpira and Chambasom finally made it to the city. Nachau and Akio welcomed them. The day after, Lisami and others went to the hospital. Tension was high among the Ntulo family members. Ntulo and Yansurili were ashamed to see Lisami and others, but they still thought that the compensation could be Lisami's reason for the donation.

Before they had a meeting with Ntulo and Yansurili, Lisami called Nachau aside and gave him an envelope. "Daddy, please, keep this with you. I hope the surgery will be successful. In case it turns out otherwise, I want the note in this envelope to be part of your ministry. Read it out where you think it will be helpful."

"Don't be negative. Focus on the support you are giving," Nachau encouraged, as he took the envelope.

Lisami smiled. "Thank you for the encouragement, and all the love you and Mummy have shown me. I remain grateful to God."

"To God be the glory. You are a blessing to us."

The doctor invited Lisami, Nachau, Akio, Chambason and Kunpira into his office. Ntulo and Yansurili were already seated for a meeting. The money was supposed to be paid to Lisami before the surgery.

Lisami, Kunpira and Nachau were asked to sign some consent papers.

After that, Ntulo removed the money from a bag. "This is the money for your donation. The sum of two million Naira," he said to Lisami.

Lisami was quiet for a short time, as she looked at Ntulo and Yansurili. The atmosphere was tense. "I am not doing it for the money. You can keep it to take care of your wife. There are things that money cannot buy. I believe this is the right thing for me to do," Lisami informed Ntulo respectfully.

Ntulo and Yansurili were broken by Lisami's statement.

Nachau and Akio were also surprised, but happy at the response of Lisami.

Chambason and Kunpira were restless with Lisami's decision. They stared at the money as if to forcefully collect it.

"Are you sure you understood what you just said?" Ntulo asked anxiously.

"I am sure, sir. Supporting your wife to get better is more precious than money," she replied and turned to the doctor. "I am ready for the procedure, sir."

Ntulo held the money, pondering. They were confronted with their faulty assumption about Lisami's motive. They had never thought someone could do such a thing. The last person they would expect to do that was Lisami. "Nemesis has caught up with us," Ntulo thought aloud.

Yansurili wept bitterly at the action of Lisami. "Lisami, I am sorry over our behaviour to you. Please, forgive us. I am too ashamed to be at your mercy," she said worriedly.

"I have forgiven you people. We are all members of God's family," Lisami remarked.

Yansurili continued to cry.

"We have caused injuries to your mind, but you are here with healing to ours. We have struggled with guilt since we took you back to the village. We earlier wanted to visit and apologize to you, but our pride did not let us. We are humbled by your love," Ntulo stated thoughtfully.

"We are finally here. Let us do what we can by the grace of God to make the future better than the past," Lisami replied gently.

The doctor was also surprised at Lisami's attitude. His medical career confronted him. Many times, even in critical situations, he had insisted on money first before medical attention was given.

Nachau and Akio kept quiet, watching situations. Akio held Lisami tightly to her chest.

"I want to have a discussion with Lisami," Kunpira said.

"Now?" the doctor asked.

"Yes."

Kunpira and Lisami stood up, and went out. Nachau and others were curious about Kunpira's desire.

"Are you out of your mind?" Kunpira inquired, immediately they went out.

Lisami was quiet.

"You rejected the money that can make us rich!"

Lisami looked at Kunpira thoughtfully.

"You cannot afford to donate your kidney for free. Don't forget that Ntulo and Yansurili had maltreated you. They do not deserve your love

The scene was of confusion and weeping. Some hospital staff and patients came to the scene. Some only stared at the situation in pity, while others tried to encourage the mourners.

The news of Lisami's sacrifice spread quickly and saddened all who heard of it. Television and radio stations highlighted it, as did newspapers. Even the state Governor was interested.

Yansurili faintly called the name of Lisami five times in the process of recovery. The doctor told Ntulo that she should not be informed about Lisami until her condition was better.

When Yansurili's condition improved, she insisted to know about Lisami. Ntulo tried to avoid her questions so that the doctor will be the one to tell her, but he couldn't. He finally told her the news. She wept and repeatedly called the name of Lisami.

*

Lisami's funeral was attended by many people. Various news agencies were also there. The state television station aired it live. The Church hall that had the capacity of seating five thousand people was filled up. Canopies and plastic chairs had to be provided outside. Even with that, several people were still standing outside.

The Governor and his Commissioners were in attendance. Some heads of Church denominations, leaders of companies, non-governmental organizations, and a few others were also present.

Kunpira, Chambasom and some people from their village attended. Most of the extended family members and friends of Ntulo and Yansurili from the city, and villages were also there. Two of Yansurili's brothers living abroad also came with their wives.

Yansurili insisted on being part of the funeral service against medical advice. "It is better I die trying than stay here and miss the funeral service," she said faintly.

The doctor insisted on keeping her in bed. He tried different ways of talking to her, but Yansurili's determination was strong. Eventually, Ntulo and the doctor convinced her to stay in the hospital.

Ntulo left two of Yansurili's relatives with her in the hospital and went to the funeral service.

Different speeches were delivered by various people. The Governor, in his speech, renamed the state orphanage Lisami Home. He warned against child abuse. Any person caught would be severely punished. He also announced sponsorship for any orphan who wanted to study at the university level.

Donations by different people to the orphanage were announced in their speeches. The sermon by the pastor was short, but effective. He preached on love and forgiveness.

Nachau had earlier requested to speak last. He saw the occasion as a good opportunity to read the note Lisami had written and given to him in the hospital. When the time came, he stood up in tears. It took him a while to calm down. "Ladies and gentlemen, today is an unforgettable day. A testimony to the fact that love is greater than hate. Lisami has left a legacy of love for all of us to emulate," he said.

The people listened keenly.

"It is common at this point for us to ask many questions about why this has happened. Lisami was a kind and brilliant girl. She was a lovely member of our family. It was our hope to see her grow to maturity and be more useful to society, but we don't own our lives."

The people still listened.

"Before the surgery, Lisami gave me a note that she wrote herself. She requested that in case the surgery did not favour her, I should make the note part of my ministry. I have already read it. I felt now is the right time to read it in public," Nachau announced.

He carefully removed the letter from the envelope. The place was quiet in expectation. Many people outside the Church hall peeped through the windows.

"It reads," Nachau stated:

> Living on earth is too short to be wasted on malice, bitterness and hate. Just like me, you probably have been hurt in different ways by different people. The best option you have is to forgive. You should forgive without thinking twice about it. Love must lead us even to those we don't know. It is important to assist someone become better.

> I want to thank Mr. and Mrs. Nachau for their support. They loved me as their daughter. The Lord will reward them. I also thank Mr. Ntulo and his wife for their first interest in me that made them take me to the city. I wish Yansurili well, and I hope she will make the best use of the kidney.

> My appeal to all of us is to reach out in love to those suffering. They are within your reach for you to assist them. They too think you can assist them - that is why they come to you. Let

us remember Jesus' words, "So now I am giving you a new commandment: Love each other. Just as I have loved you, you should love each other. Your love for one another will prove to the world that you are my disciples." For those who are yet to have the right relationship with God I advise them to do so. It is the best way to live. My father, Mr. Nachau, once told me, 'There is someone's growth in forgiveness.' Till we meet again.

"Lisami has left a challenge for all of us to think about. She has demonstrated what Jesus said, 'Greater love has no one than this, that he lay down his life for his friends.' Her time on earth is over, but we have the privilege of having the right relationship with God. I want to use this moment to invite those who need to have the right relationship with God to do so before it is too late. You can do that by realizing you are a sinner, then confessing your sins and accepting Jesus as your Lord and Saviour," Nachau explained.

Ntulo and their children wept. Most of the other people were also in tears.

Gandiban, the son of Ntulo, who had molested Lisami sexually, prayed and asked God for forgiveness. Ntulo also did the same. Kunpira, Chambasom and a few others that came from their village were not left out in the conversion experience. The funeral service became a moment for conversion and revival. Many people were reconciled to God.

After the funeral, more people who heard the testimonies of conversion were also reconciled to God.

Yansurili also received Jesus as Lord and Saviour. Her health has improved greatly. After some months, Ntulo and Yansurili supported Chambasom and Kunpira with funds to start a business in the village. They also supported their children in school. Chambasom and Kunpira were very happy with the developments.

Ntulo and Yansurili had clearly understood that things can change for or against a person at any moment. They became committed to helping orphans in different places. They started a foundation known as ANOTHER CHANCE. Many orphans were able to have good education.

The story of Lisami travelled across states and some nations, impacting lives and challenging people to love and forgive one another no matter what the offence.

Scripture References

First text in Lisami's letter- John 13:34-35 NLT.

Text in Nachau's presentation- John 15:13 NIV.